Don't You Remember?

Don't You Remember?

by **LUCILLE CLIFTON**

illustrated by **EVALINE NESS**

E. P. DUTTON & CO., INC.   NEW YORK

LIBRARY OF CONGRESS CATALOGING IN PUBLICATION DATA

Clifton, Lucille, 1936–   Don't you remember?

SUMMARY: Until her birthday a young girl is convinced
everyone makes promises to her that only she remembers.

[1. Birthdays—Fiction]   I. Ness, Evaline, illus.   II. Title.
PZ7.C6224Do   [E]   73-77448   ISBN 0-525-28840-6

Published simultaneously in Canada by Clarke,
Irwin & Company Limited, Toronto and Vancouver

Printed in the U.S.A.
First Edition

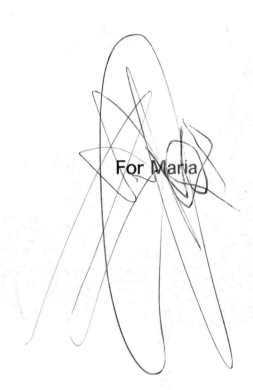

For Maria

ONCE upon a time there was a four-year-old person who remembered everything. "But I remember!" she would say. Her name was Desire Mary Tate, but she liked to be called Tate and when she grew up she was going to work at the plant just like her Daddy.

In the mornings Tate would be awake as soon as she heard the first bus pull up at the stop, and she would run into her Mama and Daddy's room and jump on the bed.

"It's next time, it's next time!" she would holler. "Wake up, it's next time!"

And usually her Daddy would turn over and say, "What's the matter with you, Tate?"

"But it's next time, Daddy," Tate would answer. "Remember you said next time you'd take me to work with you. Don't you remember?"

And usually her Daddy would just turn back over and say, "Next time, girl. Go on back to bed." And he would put the pillow on his head.

"Dag, double dag!" Tate would say when she got back into bed. She remembered everything and her Daddy didn't remember anything.

Tate's Mama worked at the bakery and her name was Desire too. She would bring home bread and cracked cookies for her family every day.

And almost every day when her Mama was walking up the front steps, Tate would open the door and holler, "Mama, did you bring it? Did you bring it?"

"Did I bring what, Desire?" her Mama would smile.

"The beautiful black cake with Tate on it in pink letters," Tate would answer. "Remember, you said you'd bring it the next time you came!"

"Oh, Desire," her Mama would always say, "go on in the house, I'll bring it next time I come home."

And Tate would stomp back into the apartment and punch her brother Marvin in the leg and say, "Dag, double dag!" real loud.

She remembered everything and her Mama just didn't remember anything.

Tate's brothers' names were Marvin and Louis and Sammy. Marvin was fifteen and his job was to take care of Tate while Mama and Daddy were at work. Next year, when Tate went to school, he was going to go back too and graduate.

Louis was thirteen and he was in the sixth grade. Sammy was twelve and he was in the sixth too.

Sometimes Marvin and Louis and Sammy would be in the kitchen talking and laughing and drinking coffee and Tate would lean on the table and whine and whine.

"Let me have some," she would whine, "I want some too. Let me have some too."

"Go on, Tate," Marvin would laugh, "you can have some later."

"But it's later now," Tate would argue.

"Go on, Tate," Marvin would say, "we didn't say you could have some now."

And Tate would give a good kick on the chair leg and holler, "Dag, double dag," while she was doing it and run off into her room.

She remembered everything and her brothers never remembered anything.

One morning Tate woke up as soon as the first bus pulled up at the stop, but she didn't run into her Mama and Daddy's room. She just lay there for a minute listening to the bus. Then she turned over and opened her eyes.

"They won't remember anyway," she whispered to herself. "They never remember anything."

Tate lay a long time watching the circles on the wallpaper twist around and fall down the corners of her room. She had just gotten to counting to nine for the third time when she heard somebody knocking on her door.

"Desire, are you all right?" It was her Mama.

"You feeling okay, Tate?" It was her Daddy.

"Go way," Tate said real loud, "you all never remember anything!"

"Come on out here, girl!" Marvin and Louis and Sammy said all together.

"Go way!" Tate hollered and pulled the sheet over her head and closed her eyes real tight.

"Poke your head out, Desire, and see," said her Mama's voice.

Tate opened her eyes and peeked her head out from under the sheet.

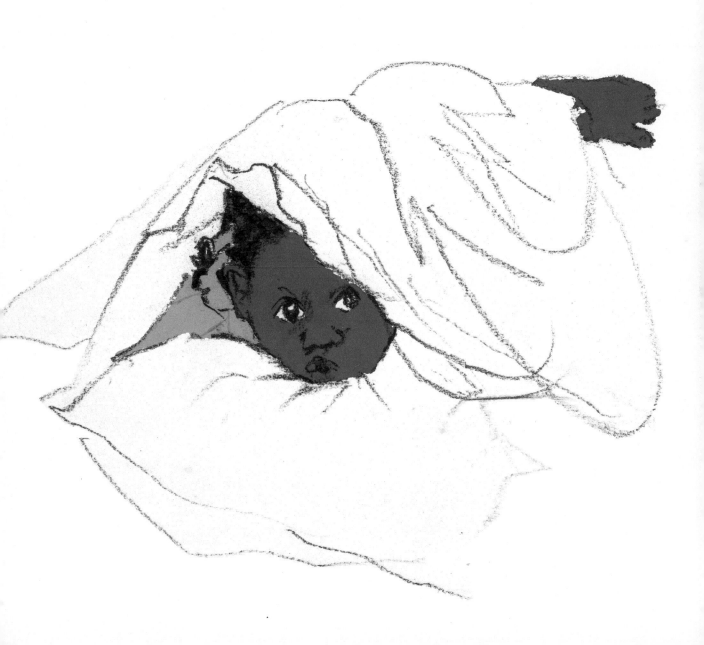

She jumped up and turned around and around on the bed! Mama was carrying a big black beautiful cake with TATE on it in pink letters!

"Come on and drink some coffee with us, girl," Marvin laughed.

"Hurry up, Tate, if you're going over to the plant with me," Daddy laughed.

"Oh, Desire, you didn't even remember your birthday," Mama laughed.

Tate leaped off the bed and ran out the bedroom door.

"Did too!" she yelled, "did too! Dag and double dag, I remember everything!"

LUCILLE CLIFTON has been writing poetry and prose for children since 1970, when *Some of the Days of Everett Anderson* (Holt), illustrated by Evaline Ness, was published. Subsequent books have been: *Everett Anderson's Christmas Coming* (Holt), *The Black B C's,* and *The Boy Who Didn't Believe in Spring.* Mrs. Clifton attended Howard University in Washington, D.C., and lives in Baltimore, Maryland, with her husband and six children.

EVALINE NESS has been illustrating children's books since 1960. She studied at the Art Institute in Chicago and the Corcoran School of Art in Washington, D.C., and was a fashion and commercial artist before she became a children's book illustrator. Miss Ness is the author/illustrator of *Sam, Bangs & Moonshine* (Holt), winner of the 1967 Caldecott Medal, *The Girl and the Goatherd,* and *Do You Have the Time, Lydia?* Miss Ness now divides her time between New York City and Palm Beach, Florida.

The text type is set in Univers 55. The book was printed by offset at Pearl Pressman Liberty.